B55 045 483 8

KU-591-228

This Walker book belongs to:

WITHDRAWN
FROM THE
ROTHERHAM
PUBLIC
LIBRARY

CITY
FARM

Let's Go to

Caryl Hart

Bee and Billy,

Billy and Bee,

See what they

can do!

WALKER BOOKS
AND SUBSIDIARIES

LONDON • BOSTON • SYDNEY • AUCKLAND

For the staff at Chatsworth Farmyard – for all the happy days~C.H. ♥▲▼ For Windmill City Farm, Bristol ~ L.T.
First published 2017 by Walker Books Ltd, 87 Vauxhall Walk, London SE11 5HJ ◆ This edition published 2019
◆ Text © 2017 Caryl Hart ◆ Illustrations © 2017 Lauren Tobia ◆ The right of Caryl Hart and Lauren Tobia to be
identified as author and illustrator respectively of this work has been asserted by them in accordance
with the Copyright, Designs and Patents Act 1988 ◆ This book has been typeset in Futura ◆ Printed in
China ◆ All rights reserved ◆ No part of this book may be reproduced, transmitted or stored in
an information retrieval system in any form or by any means, graphic, electronic or mechanical, including
photocopying, taping and recording, without prior written permission from the publisher.
British Library Cataloguing in Publication Data: a catalogue record for this book is available
from the British Library ◆ ISBN 978-1-4063-8574-8 ◆ www.walker.co.uk ◆ 10 9 8 7 6 5 4 3 2 1

the Farm!

Lauren Tobia

They're so
tumbly,
wiggly,
jumbly!
Can YOU
do it, too?

Red boots, green boots,

Swishing through the hay.

Bee and Billy

are excited...

They're on the **FARM** today!

"Look! A fluffy hen!"

shouts Bee.

She follows it

around.

It peck-peck-pecks by Billy's feet,

The crumbly crumbs

on the dusty

ground.

Billy spots a round thing,

Underneath a shed.

Gently, slowly, Bee

lifts it out...

"WOW!

Billy's found an

EGG!"

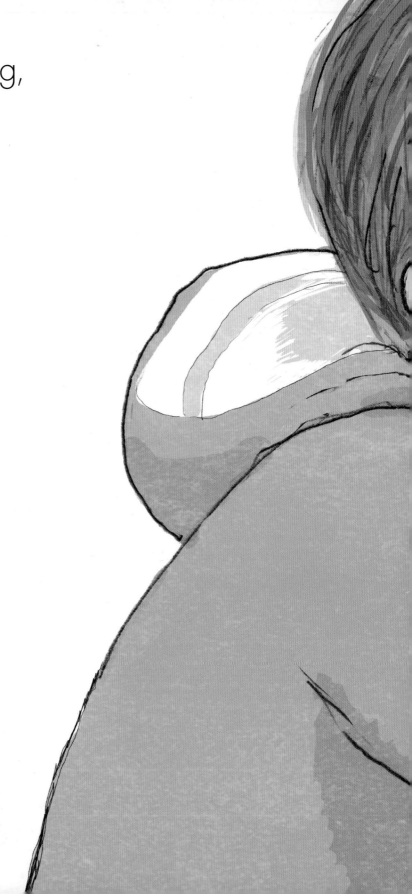

Wriggling piglets in a pen,

How many can you see?

Mummy piggy grunt-grunt-grunts,

Piglets cry, **"Squee s-q-u-e-e!"**

"Now it's time to feed the lambs!"

Bee holds a bottle tight.

But Billy clings onto his Mummy,

"Don't worry. It's all right."

Bee's little lamb is hungry,

It pulls the bottle hard.

Lamb's tail wriggles, Billy giggles,

As Bee chases it round the yard!

Can you spot the guinea pigs?

They're playing hide-and-seek!

Hopping, popping, through the hay,

Chitter-chatter-squeak!

Bee sits down on the scratchy straw,

A soft towel on her knee.

"My guinea pig's called Puzzle.

Stroke her gently, Billy.

See?"

It's noisy in the hen house,
Hens flap and cluck
and scratch.

Billy finds more eggs under a lamp...
Crick! Crack! One's going to hatch!

"**Who's inside the barn?**" asks Bee.

Calves gaze with gentle eyes.

Wet noses glisten,

long tongues poke out,

LICK!

What a surprise!

Over at the picnic bench,

Mums rummage for a snack.

But Billy isn't hungry,

"Billy! Wait!

Come back!"

"Here I am!" calls Billy.

"I'm bringing in the hay!"

Bee clambers up to help him,

And they play, and play,

and play.

Bee and Billy
   are going home,
Today has been such fun.
They're yawny, sleepy,
   snuggly, tired...

Goodbye,
everyone!

Also illustrated by Lauren Tobia:

978-1-4063-3841-6

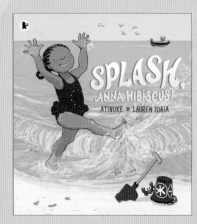

978-1-4063-5468-3

978-1-4063-7807-8

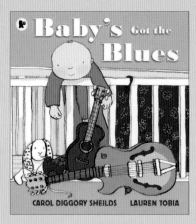

978-1-4063-6004-2

Caryl Hart is the author of more than thirty books for children.
She lives on top of a windy hill in the Peak District with her husband and two daughters.
Find her online at **carylhart.com** and on Twitter as **@carylhart1**.

Lauren Tobia lives in Bristol with her husband and their two Jack Russell terriers, Poppy and Tilly.
Find her online at **laurentobia.com** and on Twitter and Instagram as **@laurentobia**.

Available from all good booksellers

www.walker.co.uk